For Boo
E.G.

First published in hardback in Great Britain in 2017 by Boxer Books Limited.
www.boxerbooks.com

Boxer® is a registered trademark of Boxer Books Limited

A catalogue record of this book is available from the British Library.
The illustrations were prepared using hand-printed paper and acrylic paints.
The text is set in American Typewriter.
ISBN 978-1-910716-24-3
1 3 5 7 9 10 8 6 4 2
Printed in China
All of our papers are sourced from managed forests and renewable resources.

Chuffa Chuffa Choo Choo

Emma Garcia

Boxer Books

Chuffa Chuffa

4 3 2

. . . here comes the train!

Choo Choo

Clickety clack on the track.
Going to . . .

. . . the
seaside.

We can
taste the
ice cream.

here comes the train!

Clickety clack
on the track.
Going to . . .

. . . the **forest**.

We can hear
the **birds sing**.

2

Chuffa Chuffa Choo Choo

here comes the train!

Clickety clack on the track.
Going to . . .

We can see the **tall buildings**.

Chuffa Chuffa Choo Choo

here comes the train!

4 3

Clickety clack on the track.

Going to . . .

. . . the **farm**.

We can smell the **farmyard**!

Chuffa Chuffa Choo Choo

here comes the train!

Clickety clack on the track.
Going to . . .

. . . **the station** for a nice long rest.

1 seagull

Caw

But who is making all that noise?

Fly away, birds.

Night, night, train.

See you tomorrow.